The Magic Makers

I0878633

Rebel with a Cause

How ISMAT CHUGHTAI rewrote the rules for girls

MAMTA NAINY

Illustrations by Barkha Lohia

PUFFIN BOOKS

An imprint of Penguin Random House

PUFFIN BOOKS

Puffin Books is an imprint of the Penguin Random House
group of companies whose addresses can be
found at global.penguinrandomhouse.com

Published by Penguin Random House India Pvt. Ltd
4th Floor, Capital Tower 1, MG Road,
Gurugram 122 002, Haryana, India

Penguin
Random House
India

First published in Puffin Books by Penguin Random House India 2024

10 9 8 7 6 5 4 3 2 1

This book is, as the author claims, a work of 'fictionalized non-fiction' that straddles the line between facts and fiction. While it's inspired by the character herein, some of the events in the story are imagined or are creative interpretations. All names, save where obviously genuine, are fictitious and any resemblance to persons living or dead is wholly coincidental. The book does not intend to cause offence to any individual, community, or group of persons of any gender, religion, caste or linguistic identity.

ISBN 9780143466819

Book design and layout by Samar Bansal
Typeset in Quicksand
Printed at Aarvee Promotions, India

www.penguin.co.in

For budding magic-makers everywhere . . .

Uwaaa! Waa! Wa

a!

In the heartland of Uttar Pradesh,
a baby girl was born.

Her two bright eyes shone
as her two tiny fists opened
and closed.

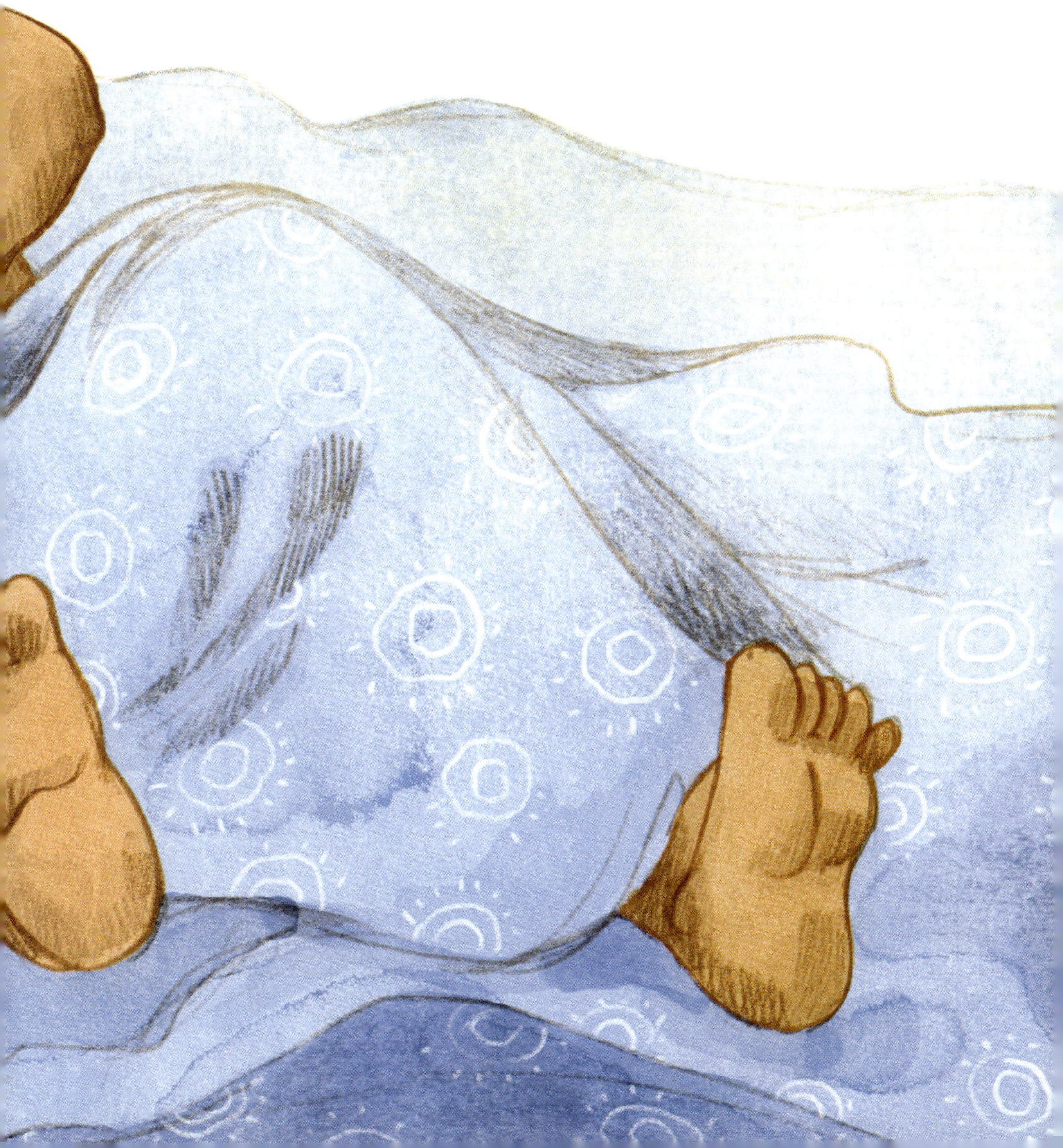

She was the ninth child
in a family of ten children.

Hers was a big family, with
aapas and bhaijaans,
dadis and dadus,
naanis and nanus,
phupis and khalus,
mumanis and mamus.

And they all affectionately
called her Chunni.

Right from the time when Chunni was a toddler, her favourite word was 'why'.

'Abba, why is the sky blue and the grass green?'

'Why can't I look at the sun for long?'

'Why does the moon walk with us?'

Why? Why? Why?

And the 'whys' only seemed to grow as Chunni was growing up.

'Amma, why does Abba go to work while you stay at home?'

'Why can't I have short hair?'

'Why does Bhai wear a *patloon* and I don't?'

'Why doesn't my dress have pockets?'

'Why can't I laugh out loud?'

Just like all kids,
Chunni loved to play.

But what she loved even more was playing the games her brothers played.

'Don't climb the trees, Chunni!'

I will!

'Don't play gilli-danda, Chunni!'

I will!

'Don't fly kites, Chunni!'

I will!

I will!

I will!

Chunni's father had a white horse. Every day, a coach came to teach her brothers how to ride. All her brothers took turns riding the horse.

Let's trot!

Move on!

One day, Chunni saw her brothers riding the snowy white horse . . .

Such a beautiful horse!
How nice it would be if I could
ride him too, she thought.

She went straight to her mother.

'I, too, want to ride the horse!' Chunni said.

'You can't, beta,' Amma replied.

'Why not, Amma?'

'Because girls don't ride horses, my child,' Amma told Chunni.

‘Says who?
And why can’t
girls ride horses?’
Chunni was not
happy with the
answer.

'What do you mean "why"?' Amma said, a bit irritated. 'Because girls have to do other things.'

'Like needlework, cooking and cleaning?' Chunni asked. 'Why don't you tell my bhais to do these things and let me ride the horse for a change?'

Amma paused her needlework.

'They do their thing, and you must do yours,' she said sternly.

'And stop arguing so much for Allah's sake! Never seen a child like this . . . Just won't give in!' Amma muttered as she left the room.

Chunni did not protest immediately, but she had many questions in her mind.

During mealtime that day, she was still thinking about what Amma had said.

Aren't girls and boys equal?
Can't girls do what boys can?

Even before going to bed, she wondered why things were so unfair.

Chunni asked herself a whole lot of questions. But the answers did not come, even when she tried. This made her more and more sure of what she had to do.

Early next morning, Chunni's Abba was reading the newspaper on the veranda.

'Abba, can I ask you something?' Chunni said.

'What is it?' asked Abba, looking over the rim of his reading glasses.

'Why can't I ride the horse?' Chunni asked.

'You wouldn't be able to, beta,' Abba replied.

'How can you be sure, Abba?'

Chunni asked.

'Unless I try, how would you know whether I will be able to ride it or not?'

Chunni's father looked at his
daughter's determined face and then . . .

Hahahahahahahahahahahahah

. . . he burst out laughing!
'It's easier to let you ride the horse than answer all your questions, my lovely little girl.'

aha!!

The next morning, when the coach came . . .

'From today, Chunni will also learn horse riding,' Abba told the coach.

Why?
How?

Mounted on the horse's back,
Chunni felt she had conquered the world!

Do you know who Chunni grew up to be?

This rebel became Ismat Chughtai, one of India's best-known Urdu writers.

At a time when books were full of rules on how women should sit, stand, laugh, talk and behave, Ismat boldly challenged these standards through her writing.

She gave a voice to millions of girls, inspiring them to stand up for themselves—just like little Chunni did.

ISMAT CHUGHTAI

FEISTY, FIERCE AND FEARLESS

Ismat Chughtai was born in 1911 in Budaun, which was a part of the United Provinces (current-day Uttar Pradesh) under British India. Lovingly called Ismat Apa, she was a bold person who did what she believed was right. A hundred years ago, women in India were not allowed to say or do what they really wanted to. But that never stopped Ismat Apa. She was afraid of no one and nothing.

At the age of fifteen, she faced opposition from many relatives but convinced her parents to let her continue her studies. She finished her BA at Isabella Thoburn College in Lucknow. Her desire to learn more didn't stop there. She even got a teacher training degree from Aligarh Muslim University.

During her time at the university, Ismat Apa began writing stories that would later make her a famous writer. A great storyteller, Ismat Apa is considered a pillar of modern Urdu literature. She was among the first writers to tell women's stories at a time when women were treated unfairly because of their gender. Ismat Apa wrote about women's lives, their struggles, dreams and ambitions. She believed that women's stories were as important as men's, and she wanted the world to hear them. Without Ismat Apa, these tales would have remained untold and unheard.

Ismat Apa believed that books and literature could bring about positive changes in society. She worked tirelessly to shed light on the lives of those who were neglected. People laughed at her and criticized her for writing about things that were considered unacceptable in those days. But Ismat Apa refused to be silenced. She kept writing fearlessly about the issues that mattered to her, with both courage and compassion.

Before she became a writer, Ismat Apa used to be a great teacher. She believed that all games were for children and that they had no gender. This, as you read in the story earlier, was something she had discovered quite early on. The horse-riding incident brought out the rebel in her, making her a rebel with a cause. Even as a child, she stood up for what she thought was right, and that decision changed her life. She didn't know then that her strong conviction in herself and her thoughts would make her a champion of women's rights. At that moment in time, she was a little girl who just wanted to ride a snowy white horse.

ACKNOWLEDGEMENTS

It truly takes a village to bring a book to life. And I am ever so grateful for the enthusiasm and expertise of some of the most wonderful people without whom this book would not have been possible. My heartfelt thanks to . . .

Sohini Mitra for believing in the story and for her steady editorial presence.

Shabari Choudhury for her editorial finesse and fine eye for detail.

Barkha Lohia for imagining this story with me and bringing it alive with her brilliant art.

Samar Bansal for his design wizardry.

My family and friends who keep my life interesting and fuel my creative interests.

And finally, to all the writers, poets, artists, musicians who have seeded my writing and thinking over the years. My tenderest hope is that some of their stories in this series find a home in a few hearts and spin some magic there.

READ MORE IN THE SERIES

Roshan's Road to Music

How Annapurna Devi began her magnificent journey into music

Mamta Nainy

'But the one sound that Roshan couldn't get enough of was the sound of Baba's sarod.'

Right from her childhood, Annapurna Devi, born as Roshanara Khan, had an ear for music. She found rhythm and melody in the most mundane sounds. She listened with wonder to the koel cooing and her grandmother snoring.

But when her father gave sarod lessons to her brother, Roshan was moved to make music of her own. How did Roshan embark on her musical journey?

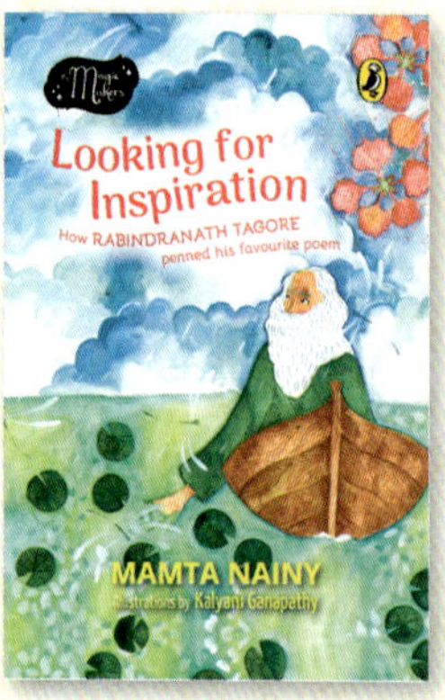

Looking for Inspiration

How Rabindranath Tagore penned his favourite poem

Mamta Nainy

'Robi started looking for Inspiration. Where could she be?'

Right from his childhood, Rabindranath Tagore, also known as Robi, was attracted to nature. He found his poetic inspiration amidst the glassy waters of the pond, the leafy trees in his garden and the endless blue sky.

But when Inspiration went missing one fine morning, Robi searched and searched all around the house. How would he write his poems again?

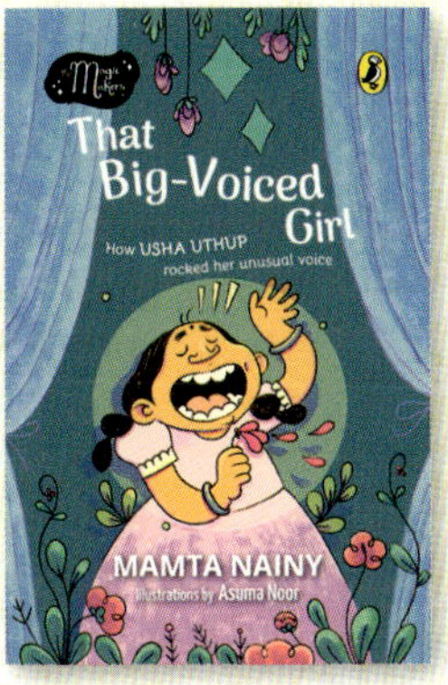

That Big-Voiced Girl

How Usha Uthup rocked her unusual voice

Mamta Nainy

'There's no one way every girl should sound, is there?'

Right from her childhood, Usha Uthup knew that music was her true calling. She picked up songs from the radio and sang in her big, booming voice.

But when rejected during the audition for her school choir, Usha wondered if her unusual voice was any good. All she wanted was to sing. Does she find a way?

Baloo's Big Win

How Palwankar Baloo broke the caste barrier in cricket

Mamta Nainy

'Does anyone really win when not everyone gets to play?'

Right from his childhood, Baloo loved cricket. But he lived at a time when the rules of the game weren't fair. Despite being a great bowler, he wasn't allowed on the team because he was from a lower caste. Not one to give up easily, Baloo worked hard and was eventually picked to play on the team.

But even after this, he wasn't allowed to mix freely with his teammates. Could Baloo overcome this obstacle and change the game of cricket?

Mamta Nainy is a writer based in New Delhi. She has authored over thirty books for children, many of which have gone on to win national and international awards and recognition. She also works as a literary translator, translating primarily from English to Hindi, with several published works of translation. Mamta is inspired by the unfettered imagination of children and loves travelling but is too lazy to do it. So, she mostly makes do with reading.

Barkha Lohia is an artist and illustrator from India, now based in Toronto, Canada. Her work is an amalgamation of everything experienced around her, be it the bustling railway stations, boisterous characters in streets or the quiet solitude experienced in midst of nature. Working across both traditional and digital mediums, her approach is to keep the tone and texture of her work organic. She enjoys working on varied themes, but characters deeply rooted in the natural world, as well as humorous stories often find a place in her work. When she is not creating, she enjoys being outside, collecting, loitering and sketching.